ELEVATOR SHAFT

AN EROTIC ADVENTURE

VICTORIA RUSH

VOLUME 19

JADE'S EROTIC ADVENTURES - BOOK 19

COPYRIGHT

Spying on the neighbors just got a lot more interesting...

Everything's sexier in the dark...

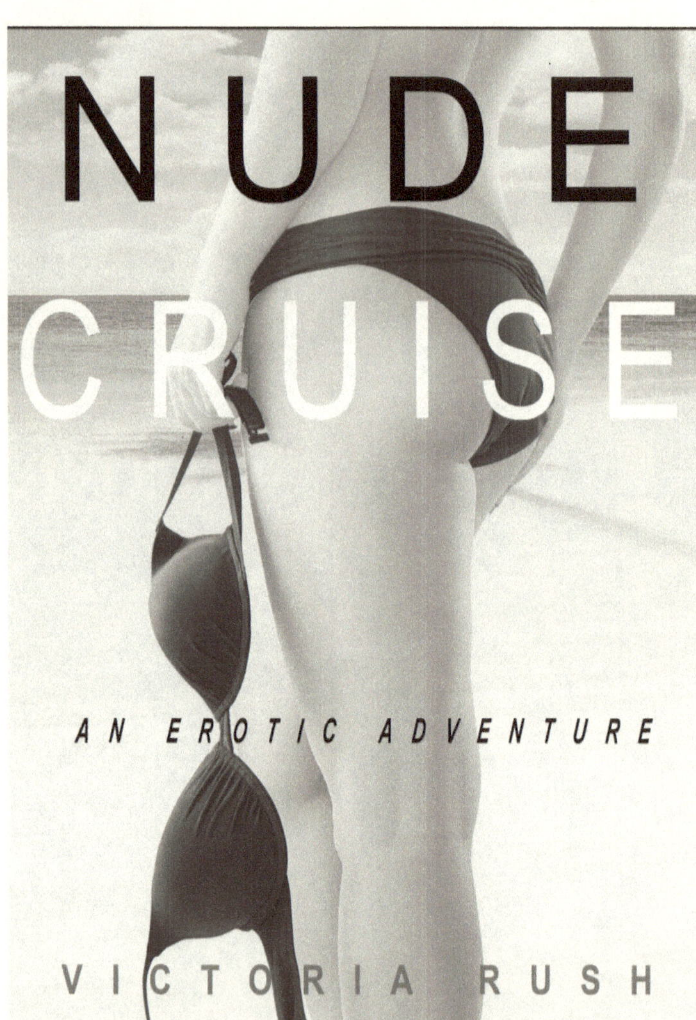

Some people get wet on a cruise for different reasons...

Books 1 -5 in the bestselling series - 60% off

For the uninhibited...

1

———

I breathed a sigh of relief as I stepped into the elevator just after 5 p.m. on the day before Thanksgiving. My meeting with the creative director of Ogilvy & Mather Advertising had gone better than expected, and I felt elated at the prospect of working with the prestigious agency. We'd taken longer than anticipated to discuss the particulars of their Disney Studios campaign, but at the end of the day he'd awarded me exclusive rights to design all their new movie posters.

The view from their penthouse suite atop the Willis Tower was breathtaking. Chicago had been enjoying an unusually mild November, and I could see all the way across Lake Michigan on the clear autumn day. They'd feted me with a late luncheon in the Skydeck Restaurant on the 103rd floor and although I felt fully sated, I was looking forward to the annual feast with my family over the long weekend.

Ogilvy's offices had cleared out early in advance of the weekend crush, and I nodded toward the two lone elevator occupants as the door slid closed behind us. They were both dressed in expensive suits and looked to be about my age.

The man standing to my right had thick ruffled hair, dark eyes, and broad shoulders that curved nicely in his tight wool suit.

But it was the woman standing on the other side of the elevator that caught my attention. Standing almost six feet tall in her Louboutin pumps, her perfectly manicured brows arched over aquamarine-colored eyes and red pouty lips. Like the handsome hunk on the opposite side of the elevator, her busty figure left little to the imagination in her form-fitting skirt and blazer. My pussy twitched as I glanced downward, eyeing her long and shapely legs. Given how far they were standing apart and how hard they were working to avoid eye contact, I quickly surmised that they didn't know each other.

Funny how perfect strangers always find the quickest way to separate themselves in close quarters, I thought.

I glanced at the elevator console to confirm the ground floor button was selected, then I stepped to the back of the lift to get a closer look at the two passengers. They looked even sexier from behind, as I shamelessly ran my eyes over their figures. The man had a nice round bump lifting the back of his blazer, and I could make out the muscular curve of his thighs filling in his tight-fitting pants.

I bet that guy doesn't have much trouble getting his share of the action, I thought, suddenly feeling warm under my form-fitting suit.

But the woman's suit was even tighter, displaying every curve and valley of her sexy figure. As I stared at the globes of her firm ass clearly delineated in her snug skirt, my panties began to moisten thinking about how much I'd like to lick my way up her long legs all the way from her pretty feet to her steamy pussy.

Normally I tried to respect everyone's desire for privacy

while traveling on elevators, but whether it was the after-effects of my three-martini lunch or my giddiness from landing the prestigious account, for some reason I felt the need to break the awkward silence in the lift.

I hope you guys have as good a reason as I did to work this late on Thanksgiving weekend," I said.

"Par for the course," the man said, turning his head halfway around and smiling half-heartedly in my direction. "Goes with the territory, unfortunately."

"Mmm," the lady grunted, staring impassively toward the front of the elevator. "No rest for the wicked in the urban jungle."

I peered back and forth between the two strangers, sensing some tension between them. Were they ex-lovers or disgruntled co-workers? Maybe they'd just been working late on a problem account and were exhausted after another long day at the office.

"Do you both work at Ogil–" I said, hoping to make some new introductions at the firm.

But as the pressure increased in my ears from the rapid descent of the elevator, suddenly the lights went out and the lift screeched to an abrupt halt.

"What the–" the woman said, breathing heavily.

"Oh my God!" I said, clutching my briefcase next to me as I quivered in the darkness. "What's going on?"

"It's probably just a power failure," the man said. "Everybody's been gearing up for the holidays and the little heat wave has been drawing a lot of power from the grid lately. I'm sure ComEd will have us back on track in no time."

"Are we safe, stuck so far off the ground?" I said nervously. "This is my worst nightmare – being stuck in an elevator suspended hundreds of feet in the air."

"Not to worry," the man reassured. "Modern elevators are

equipped with multiple fail-safe mechanisms. An emergency brake automatically engages in the event of a power failure, so there's no way it can drop any further."

"What about the *cables*?" I asked, still petrified at the thought of losing control over the elevator. "Is there a chance they might fatigue or snap if this goes on for a while?"

"No way," he said. "There's more than one cable holding us up and each one is rated for much higher loads than our current weight. As strange as it may sound, this might be one of the safest places to be in the middle of a blackout. I hate to think how crazy it might be on the *streets* right now with all the traffic lights out."

"That's a small consolation," I said, beginning to breathe a little more normally. "I'd rather take my chances out there in broad daylight instead of being cooped up in this claustrophobic death trap."

In the pitch blackness, I could hear the sound of the woman's hands sliding frantically over the blacked-out console.

"What do we do now?" she said. "Can we communicate with somebody while we're locked up in here? I can't find the emergency call button in the dark–"

Suddenly, the screen of the man's cell phone illuminated and I saw his fingers tapping the surface. A flashlight lit up on the back side, and he pointed it toward the elevator control panel.

"This should help a bit," he said.

We could see a red button near the bottom of the console, and the woman slammed her palm against it repeatedly.

"Can anyone hear me?" she screamed. "We're stuck in an elevator near the top floor of the Willis Tower. Somebody help us, please!"

"The coms are probably down too," the man said calmly. "None of the electronic systems will be working as long as the power is down. I think we just need to wait it out until power is restored or the building's maintenance crew comes to retrieve us."

"Our phones," the woman said, turning her head in the direction of the man's glowing screen. "There are other ways we can call for help."

The two of us pulled our phones out of our purses and tapped 911. A message filled the screen indicating that the mobile network was temporarily unavailable.

"What the fuck?" the woman said. "The *phones* aren't working either?"

As the man lifted his phone to examine his screen, the backlight illuminated his handsome face.

"There's no bars. The power failure has probably disabled the cell towers too."

"Doesn't the phone company have back-up generators or something?" the woman said.

"Yes, but it will likely take some time for their systems to come online. But even if they do, every person in Chicago will likely be calling their family or emergency services to make sure everything is okay. I don't expect we'll be able to make any calls for at least a couple of hours."

"A couple of *hours*?!" the woman exclaimed. "How are we going to survive in this cramped elevator that long? What about air? Won't we run out of oxygen before then?"

"We're going to be fine, Elle," the man said. "There's plenty of ventilation ducts in the compartment, and with fifty floors above and below us, there's enough oxygen in the elevator shaft to support us for quite a long time."

So they do know each other, I smiled.

"You seem to know a lot about elevators for a guy wearing such an expensive suit," I said.

"Working on the hundred and fifth floor of the tallest building in the Midwest will do that to a guy. I'm a little claustrophobic too, so I did a little bit of research before I took this job. We'd *starve* to death long before any malfunction of the elevator would kill us."

"So we just stand here twiddling our thumbs while we wait for someone to come save us?" I said.

"It looks that way. But I'm guessing the emergency response people have their hands full dealing with a city full of panicked citizens. Plus, there's lots of other elevators in this building, so it's likely to be at least a few hours before anyone comes to our rescue. You might want to sit down and relax to make the wait a little more comfortable."

The man squatted toward the floor then leaned back against the wall and straightened his legs out in front of him. Recognizing that we might be in this for a long haul, I followed his cue and sat down kitty-corner to him against the back wall. Peering up at the woman, I saw that she was still tapping the surface of her phone, trying to make an outside connection.

"Why don't you make yourself more comfortable, Elle?" I said, trying to ease her distress. "My name's Jade. I didn't catch your name–"

"West," the man said. "The least we can do is try to get to know one another better while we're stuck in here. Make the best of an uncomfortable situation."

"It's either that or play Candy Crush on our phones until the power comes back on," I joked.

Elle exhaled a sigh of resignation as I watched her phone slide down the wall to my right while she plopped down on the floor.

"Why not?" she said. "I can't think of a better inmate to spend my time with while I'm locked up in here.".

"You two know one another then," I said. "Do you work together, or do you have some kind of *other* relationship?"

"Hardly," Elle huffed. "Not in a million years."

"We work together at Ogilvy," West said. "We handle two of the firm's largest accounts. I guess there's been a bit of a competition of sorts to see who would make partner first–"

"Not likely, with that lame-ass automotive account you've been handed. Can't you see that's a dying business with more and more people switching to foreign cars these days?"

"Maybe, but at least it's *reliable*. Not like that new tech account of yours–"

Suddenly, our conversation was interrupted with the sound of banging coming from inside the elevator shaft.

"What's that noise?" Elle said.

We paused to listen as the clanging sound grew louder and more frenetic.

"Could it be the maintenance technicians trying to open the doors above us?" I said.

"Unlikely," West said. "I can't imagine they'd be able to respond this fast. Most of them are probably stuck in traffic on their way home already."

"What is it then?" Elle asked. "Are the cables about to snap?"

The clanging noises suddenly changed to a rhythmic pattern of short and long taps.

"It sounds like an SOS signal. Probably from another group of people trapped in an elevator above or below us."

"That's not a bad idea," Elle said, pounding her fist against the wall beside her. "At least we know we've got some company."

"Not that it's likely to do us much good," West said.

"There's not much either of us can do from our current locations."

Elle tilted her phone up, scanning the ceiling with her flashlight.

"If you're so clever Mr. Smartypants, maybe you can figure out how to get the lid off this thing and find a nearby exit?"

West chuckled softly in the darkness.

"There's a reason these things aren't designed to be evacuated from the inside," he said. "It takes a special key to open the lid from the outside. It wouldn't be safe for us to exit that way even if we could. Who knows when the elevator might start up again and pin us against the walls?"

"With all the time you spend in the gym," Elle huffed, "I would have thought you could jimmy up the cables to the nearest door."

"Yeah," West said. "I'm sure it's that simple. I'll get right on it."

It was obvious there was a lot more going on between these two than a competitive rivalry. Their little digs sounded more like a high school crush than a workplace disagreement.

"Is it getting hot in here, or is it just me?" I said, trying to break the tension.

I'd begun to perspire under my suit, and I was pretty sure it wasn't because I was afraid of plummeting to my death anymore.

"I feel it too," West said. "The air conditioning systems would have gone offline along with the power. And the radiant heat from outside the building is slowly creeping into the elevator shaft."

"Oh great," Elle said. "So now we're going to *boil* to death while we wait for help?"

"It shouldn't get much hotter than the temperature outside. I expect it will begin to cool as the sun goes down. You can always loosen your clothes to get more comfortable."

"That's the best pick-up line I've heard in a while," I chuckled.

"You have *no* idea," Elle sneered. "He's full of them."

"I guess it wouldn't hurt to take off my jacket and loosen my shirt," I said. "It's not like we can *see* anything in the pitch dark anyway, right?"

"I wouldn't put it past him to flash his phone you least expect it," Elle said. "We still have a few fleeting sources of power while we're waiting."

"Not for long," West said, peering at the glowing surface of his phone. "I'm already in the yellow zone for power. How about you guys?"

"I'm showing ten percent," I said.

"I'm down to *two* percent," Elle cursed. "I knew I should have replaced my battery during the last upgrade cycle. I can barely get through a full day at the best of times."

"We're consuming a lot of extra juice with our screens and flashlights on full strength," West said. "It's probably best to turn them off or at least switch to sleep mode to save them for when we really need them."

"Awesome," Elle said. "What do we do in the meantime?"

"Why don't we do what people used to do before the advent of modern technology and *talk* to one another," I said. "It sounds like you guys could use some more open lines of communication anyhow."

"What did you want to talk about?" she said sarcastically. "Our favorite hobbies and the unusual weather we've had lately?"

"Well it's probably best to steer clear of work," I

suggested. "Tell us something personal about yourself, something nobody else would know. I mean, I'll probably never see you guys again once we get out of this predicament. Who else is gonna know?"

The compartment suddenly fell quiet as each of us pondered what to say.

"You know, it's strange," West said, breaking the silence. "I've always wondered what it would be like be in a situation like this. It's kind of *exciting* in a way, being left to our own devices without any outside stimulation."

"Kind of like being trapped on a deserted island," Elle chuckled.

"In a way, I guess. Makes you wonder what you'd do to pass the time, so far removed from modern conveniences."

"What do you think *you'd* do to amuse yourself on this deserted island, West?" I said, eager to steer the conversation in a different direction.

"Depends on who I was stranded with."

"What if it were just *you*?"

"I guess I'd have to scrape by on my memories. Or spend my time fantasizing about how to get off the island."

"And if you couldn't?" Elle said. "What would you fantasize about then?

"The usual macho stuff, I suppose. "That I was stranded in paradise with a supermodel–"

"Or two?" I joked.

"The more the merrier," West said.

"You men are always fantasizing about doing it with multiple women at the same time," Elle said.

"What about you then, Elle?" I asked, deflecting the attention away from West temporarily. "What would be *your* ultimate fantasy if you were stranded on a deserted island?"

"I'd probably go stir crazy all by myself after a while. I

suppose I wouldn't be much different from West, dreaming about being stuck there with David Beckham or Brad Pitt..."

"Only *men*?" I said, fishing for more details.

"I dunno. I've never tried it with women before. But I suppose if we were stuck on a deserted island long enough, one thing might lead to another..."

"What about you, Jade?" West said, sensing a theme developing.

"I lean more toward women, myself. Although if I didn't have any other choice, I might be tempted to dabble a bit–"

"It *is* getting hot in here," West said as the sound of rustling clothes filled the compartment.

"Hotter than your deserted island fantasy?" I asked.

"It's getting there. All this talk about mixing it up with different partners is making me hot under the collar."

"Don't let us stop you from acting out your fantasy, West," Elle said. "It's just us girls in here. We won't tell if you don't."

"What exactly did you have in mind?" West asked.

"Something tells me you're getting uncomfortable in those heavy clothes for more than one reason," she said. "If you need to free the beast, don't let us stop you from getting your freak on."

"Um..." West paused, unsure if we were thinking the same thing.

"I think maybe West needs a little extra encouragement, Elle," I said. "Why don't you scooch up a little closer to me so he can exercise his fantasy more vividly?"

"This little adventure is getting more interesting by the moment," Elle purred, shimmying her hips across the floor to sit next to me. "I suppose there's more than *one* way to relieve the boredom when you're stuck in an elevator."

2

———

"So, West..." I said, hoping to capitalize on the rapidly developing heat in the room. "Tell us more about your little fantasy. Maybe it'll help keep our minds off this unpleasant situation we find ourselves in."

"Um, well," he said, happy to have a distraction to mask his real desires. "I guess I'd have to get to know these supermodels a bit better before we got down to business. I'd have to loosen them up a little before they thought about having sex with me, let alone with each other."

"Oh?" I said, playing along. "What would you want to know about us – I mean *them* – in order to get them in the mood?"

"I dunno, something about their families, I suppose. Maybe their relationship status. I'd need to make sure they were unattached before I proposed any kind of physical engagement. They might be kind of shy about wanting to try anything if they were already in a committed relationship."

"Let's pretend *we're* your fantasy supermodels for a moment," I said, nudging Elle's thigh playfully. "Let's see just how good your pick-up lines really are."

West shifted uncomfortably on the elevator floor and cleared his throat, imagining himself in a bar wedged between two women.

"Okay..." he said. "Well, first, of course, I'd ask them their names."

"I'm Jade," I purred.

"Elle," my partner-in-crime giggled.

"I'm West. Bit of a pickle we've gotten ourselves into. I suppose the first thing we need to do is make sure we have enough food and water to get us through this unfortunate turn of events. We don't know how long this situation might last."

"I've got a candy bar in my purse," I said, pretending to ruffle through my belongings.

"And I've got some bottled water," Elle said.

"That won't get us very far," West said. "But we might be able to catch some fish and create a pit to store fresh water when it rains. I guess our next order of business is to figure out how to send a signal to a passing ship so someone knows we're here. Do either of you carry a lighter?"

"I'm afraid I don't smoke," I said.

"Neither do I," Elle said.

"That's funny," West chuckled. "I always said that would be a deal-breaker whenever I met a pretty girl, but in this case we're going to have to find a workaround..."

"Are you saying you think we're *pretty*?" I teased.

"Well I don't want to swell your heads, but if I have to be stuck on this island for an extended period of time, I can't imagine two people I'd rather be with."

He's not bad, I whispered in Elle's ear.

He's got his moments, she nudged.

"So how are we going to let anyone know we're here then?" I said.

West rustled through his suit jacket and I heard a soft tinkling sound.

"I should be able to use my reading glasses as a magnifying lens to start a fire. Then we just need to find some fresh foliage or wet logs to create enough smoke..."

"You seem to know a lot about survival techniques for a guy who works in an office all day long," Elle huffed.

"Maybe I watch a little too much of that show Man vs. Wild."

"Well if you think you can get us out of this situation, we'd be willing to do just about anything you asked," she purred.

"Including eating bugs and drinking your own urine?"

"I'm pretty sure we can find something a little more palatable to eat between the three of us," I said, squeezing Elle's thigh.

"It's too bad we've gotten ourselves into this predicament so close to the holiday," West said. "You both must have been looking forward to enjoying a proper Thanksgiving meal with your families."

"I was just going to have an informal get-together with a few of my siblings at my mother's place," I said.

"What about you, Elle?" West said, fishing for more details about his colleague. "What did you have planned for the holidays?"

"I was on my way to the airport to visit my folks in LA when we got stuck in here. I hope they don't worry too much when they don't hear from me."

"Is there anyone *else* who'll be concerned about your whereabouts?"

Smooth, I nudged Elle. *He's looking to see if you're unattached.*

It was becoming increasingly obvious that West had more than just a working interest in her.

"Other than my *boss*, you mean?" Elle kidded. "Unfortunately, my job doesn't afford much free time for extra-curricular activities. What about you?" she said, turning back to West. "Who were *you* planning to spend some quality time with over the holidays?"

I smiled in the darkness, happy to hear the walls breaking down between the two co-workers.

"Other than my roommate and a few buddies on our house-league hockey team? We were just going to order a pizza and sit down to watch some football over the long weekend."

"You sound like a dyed-in-the-wool bachelor," Elle mused. "I didn't picture you sharing a flat with a buddy."

"Chicago's an expensive city for a single guy. Besides, sometimes it helps to have a wingman to navigate the social jungle. Speaking of living arrangements, it might be a good idea to start looking for a comfortable spot to spend the night–"

"We've already got plenty of shelter in our little corner under the palm trees," I kidded. I shifted my weight, feigning discomfort. "Although it *is* a little hard. I could use a pillow about now..."

West folded up his jacket and passed it toward me in the dark, and I placed it under Elle's knees, nodding appreciatively.

He's a gentleman too, I whispered, trying to encourage their reluctant courtship.

"So you're a *player*, then," she said, still unconvinced. "Where do you and your buddy bring your conquests when you want to have a little fun? Isn't it a bit cramped in your two-bedroom apartment? Or do you two create your own fun with each other?"

"Uh, *no*," West said. "I don't swing that way. What about you two? What are two pretty girls like you doing still single? I might say the same thing about you."

"Oh I like *men* alright," Elle said. "I just haven't found one yet worthy of my attention."

"What kind of man are you looking for?" West probed.

"The strong silent type, I suppose. Someone who knows how to treat a woman like a lady and is good with his hands..."

"Like someone who could get you out of a jam like this?"

"Possibly. But someone who's also a good lover and provider. He'd have to have a stable job and a good build..."

"Fair enough," West said, looking to bring me back into the fold. "How about you Jade? What are you looking for in a potential partner?"

"Someone with long slender legs who can wrap herself around my hips while I fuck her madly–"

"Jesus," West said, adjusting his equipment in the dark. "I've always wondered how you women do that exactly. How you make love without a–"

"*Penis*? Don't tell me you haven't watched your fair share of girl-on-girl porn? We can do pretty much everything a man can do, just without all the mess."

"What about–*penetration*? Don't you ever miss that?"

"We have lots of ways to get that when we're in the mood. Between strap-on cocks, double-sided dildos and all the special sex toys on the market, we can find plenty of ways to stimulate ourselves on both the inside and the outside. In fact, I'm carrying one in my purse right now. You never know when you might feel the need..."

"Really?" West said, his voice taking on a new sense of urgency. "Where do you use it? Isn't it kind of noisy?"

"Not this one. A friend of mine introduced me to it recently. It's called the Osé, designed by a woman. It doesn't vibrate so much as *throb*. It's incredibly lifelike, with a long undulating wand and an opening at the base that provides stimulation remarkably similar to a tongue–"

"Holy shit!" Elle interrupted. "Can I see this thing? I've never heard of a woman's vibrator like that."

"Of course," I said, happy to see that see her rapidly warming up.

I opened my purse and handed her the soft silicone instrument. She ran her hands over the long finger-shaped extension, then pressed her hand into the little hole.

"How does it work exactly?" she said. "It's not shaped like any vibrator I've ever seen."

"Feel for a little notch near the bottom of the base. There's two modes, each of which is activated with a press of the button."

Elle ran her fingers over the base of the object in the dark, then I heard her gasp.

"My God," she said. "It's *moving*. Like a real finger!"

"Exactly," I nodded. "It's designed to simulate the movement and feel of a real person. The curvature of the wand is perfect for stimulating your G-spot. Press the button again and see what *else* it can do."

I heard another click and Elle's body suddenly lurched next to mine.

"What the *fuck*?!" she exclaimed. "That feels just like a–"

"Tongue?" I said. "You won't believe how lifelike it is until you try it for real. Why don't you see for yourself?"

"Right here?!"

"Why not?" I said. "We're all getting pretty worked up

with all this talk of sex with different partners. Besides, it's not like any of us can see anything in the pitch dark. If ever there was a safe place to try something like this, this is the time."

"I don't know," Elle hesitated. "It is intriguing, but I hardly know you guys..."

"Come on," I said. "I know you want it. I can feel your hips squirming next to me. Why don't you just slip it under your skirt for a moment? I think you'll get the idea pretty quickly what it's capable of."

Elle paused for a moment, then slowly began to spread her thighs apart. I could feel her hand rustling between her legs, then she gasped.

"Right?" I said. "Not like anything you've ever tried before, is it?"

"No," she panted, spreading her thighs further apart. "It feels more like a–"

"Real person?"

"Mmm," she purred.

"It might not be quite as good as the real thing, but you'll never know until you feel it against your naked flesh. Why don't you take your clothes off? We can place West's jacket under your hips if you're worried about the dirty floor. You don't mind do you, West?"

"Definitely not," he said, unbuckling his belt.

"Maybe for just a few seconds," Elle said. "But no peeking."

"Our phones are turned off, remember? No one will have any idea what you're doing unless you tell us."

"Okay, but no comments from the peanut gallery while I try this thing out. I'm self-conscious enough without you guys taunting me in the dark..."

"Maybe if we *all* took off our clothes together, it would

make everybody feel more comfortable. That way, we could each explore our own bodies to the extent we feel comfortable. What do you think, West?"

"Way ahead of you," he said, pulling his pants down across the floor.

"Just go slow as you explore the device's capabilities," I said to Elle. "We'll be enjoying ourselves along with you."

"That does sound pretty hot actually," she said. "I'm getting hornier by the moment."

I lifted my hips off the floor, then pulled my skirt down over my legs and placed it underneath me. Then I grabbed Elle's hand and pulled it over my bare thigh, inches from my steaming pussy.

"That makes two of us," I said.

"Damn, Jade," she said. "Your skin is so warm."

"That's not the *only* part of me that's warm right now," I said. "Go ahead, let yourself loose."

Elle paused for a second, then unzipped the back of her skirt and shimmied it down over her ankles. Then she lifted her hips and pulled her panties off her legs.

"There," I said. "Doesn't that feel better? Now give our little friend a try against your bare skin."

Elle paused with the vibrator poised inches from her twitching pussy.

"Do you prefer to use the finger or the tongue?" she hesitated.

"Both, depending on my mood. Why don't you start by letting the finger caress you around your opening?"

Elle turned her hand and positioned the Osé so the finger bent toward her in rhythmic motions.

"It feels–*strange*," she said. "Like I'm being touched by a robot."

"But a very *sexy* robot, yes? Just pretend it's Brad Pitt's or David Beckham's or someone *else's* finger caressing you..."

"Mmm," she sighed, tilting her head back against the wall of the elevator. "That does feel better."

"You might want to tease yourself for a while until you get fully warmed up. When you're ready, feel free to insert it inside to experience the full capability of the toy."

"Oh, I'm getting *warmed up* alright," she panted. "How about you guys?"

I spread my legs further apart and rested my thigh overtop Elle's as I began to circle my hand over my clit. With the two of us sitting so close together, she must have felt the movement of my arm against her side as I began to stimulate myself manually.

"I'm burning up inside," I panted as the sound of my fingers rubbing against my wet labia filled the compartment. "How are you doing over there, West?"

"I'm thoroughly enjoying this fantasy," he panted. "I haven't been this hard in ages."

"I'm guessing there's something *else* hard in this room," I said, flapping my thigh against Elle's. "Why don't you put that wand inside you so you can fantasize along with us?"

I could feel Elle's arms tense up for a moment as she held the tip of the undulating finger against her opening, then she groaned, sliding down the wall. As I listened to the sound of the long appendage slipping inside her dripping pussy, I slid the fingers of my right hand inside me at the same time.

"Uhnn," she groaned, pressing the device firmer against her vulva.

"Do you *still* need Brad Pitt on your deserted island?" I said.

"Not with this thing by my side," she purred. "This is

better than any man. At least it knows the right places to caress."

"Feels heavenly, doesn't it?" I said, curling my fingers inside my own hole to rub the front side of my G-spot. "Have you turned the tongue on yet?"

"Not yet," Elle panted. "I'm just enjoying the feeling of being stroked inside right now."

"Mmm," I said, feeling my juices beginning to run down the crack of my ass. I was thrilled that Elle had loosened up enough to feel comfortable sharing what she was experiencing. "Take your time, baby. We've got all the time in the world."

"That's what worries me," she grunted. "That we might be stuck in this elevator all weekend."

"I'm sure we can find plenty of other ways to keep ourselves amused if it comes to that," I said. "But don't worry about any of that right now. Just pretend you're stranded in paradise with your ultimate lover. What would you like him to do next?"

"I'd like her to lick me," she slipped. "I mean *him*. I mean whoever."

I reached between Elle's slippery legs and tapped the button on the underside of her vibrator one more time. She pressed the device harder against her body and squealed with a guttural moan.

"Oh my God," she groaned. "That feels incredible. I feel it's tongue. It's so lifelike..."

"Yes, Elle," I purred. "Imagine it's your fantasy lover worshipping your body. You're so hot right now."

"Is this how you do it?" she said. "I mean when you're with other women? This doesn't feel like any *man* I've ever been with..."

"Like I said, the toy is designed by a woman to provide

feminine stimulation in the most erotic manner. But you'll never know what it really feels like to make love to another woman until you try–"

"*Fuck*, Jade," Elle growled. "I want to feel you against my body. This feels so good."

"Yes, baby," I whispered, lifting my hand to her chin and turning her face to meet my lips. As we began to kiss passionately, I pulled my hand out of my pussy and slipped it under her blouse, cupping her breasts and pinching her erect nipples. "Imagine it's *me* licking your clit right now."

"*Oh fuck, oh fuck*," she gasped. "I can feel it coming..."

"Yes," I purred, rolling my tongue around the inside of her mouth. "Come inside my mouth, Elle. I want to feel you twitching as I suck your button."

"Oh God!" she wailed. "I cumming, Jade! I cumming so hard. Suck my pussy!"

As we face-fucked each other imagining we were joined at the hips instead of the mouth, I heard West groan on the other side of the elevator as Elle began shaking uncontrollably against my body. Even though I hadn't touched her anywhere near her pussy, with our tongues intertwined and my hand squeezing her shaking tits, I felt incredibly connected to her. As she groaned into my mouth in the throes of a powerful climax, I suddenly gushed out of my opening, spraying my juices all over her bare legs while we quivered together in the darkness.

Something told me this was going to be just the start of our little fantasy adventure...

3

—————

For the longest time after we came, nobody said anything, as awkward silence filled the compartment. All we could hear was the sound of quiet breathing while we all recovered from our powerful climaxes. There wasn't even any rustling of clothes while we lay there in the dark, completely naked. There was something incredibly erotic about knowing each of us sat inches away from each other, with our exposed genitals still throbbing in excitement.

After a few minutes, I heard Elle reach between her legs and pull the Osé out of her wet pussy with a distinct plop.

"Thanks for letting me share your little toy," she said, handing it to me in the darkness. "I'm sorry that I've made such a mess of it..."

"Mmm," I said, placing the tip of the wand in my mouth and sucking it loudly. "Don't give it a second thought. I like it that way. You taste exquisite. I only wish I could have felt you twitching in my mouth for real."

"With that vibrator's tongue doing its action between my legs and you kissing me at the same time, it was like you were actually there," she said. "I haven't been this turned on in a long time."

"What about you, West?" I said, trying to bring our silent partner into the loop. "Did you enjoy our little fantasy role play? Do you think your supermodels are getting sufficiently warmed up?"

"Damn near," he panted. "That was the most erotic thing I've ever heard. My only regret is that nobody was actually *touching* each other."

"Oh, there was plenty of touching going on, believe me," I said. "And from the sounds of things on the other side of the elevator, you seemed to be enjoying yourself plenty enough."

"Well, yes," he said. "But it's not quite the same as–"

"Having someone *else* touch you? What do you think, Elle? Are you ready to take it to the next level?"

"Maybe," she said, hesitating. "What did you have in mind?"

"Between the three of us, with so many different, um–*tools*–to work with, there's an almost infinite number of ways we can engage. We could pair up to start, then maybe swap partners before the three of us get together. What's your pleasure?"

Elle paused for a minute as she pondered the possibilities. I sensed the walls were beginning to break down between her and West, but there was also no denying her attraction to me.

"I've always wondered what it would be like to make love to another woman," she said. "With you being so much more experienced in that area, maybe you could teach me how to do it properly..."

I grinned at Elle's feeble attempt to mask her real desires. She had no idea what she was in for.

"I can work with that," I said. "How about you, West? Do you think you can hold on a little longer while Elle and I have a bit more fun?"

"Oh, I'll be *holding on*, alright. I'm hard as a rock again knowing I'm about to realize one of my ultimate fantasies."

"Well you go right ahead and enjoy yourself over there while Elle and I get to know each other a little better."

I turned to Elle and squeezed her hand gently.

"Do you want to be the top or the bottom?"

"What do you mean?" she said. "I thought that only applied to men–"

"When two women get together, usually one takes the submissive role while the other takes a more dominant role. It's the same with lesbians as with gay men."

"Okay..." she said. "I guess since I'm the neophyte here, I should assume the more submissive role–"

"Not necessarily," I said. "If you were to take a more active role, you could proceed at your own pace and explore things as they strike your fancy."

"I kind of like the sound of that. How should we position ourselves to start?"

I paused for a moment to think about the best way to give her optimal freedom of movement while still allowing me to touch her freely.

"Why don't you kneel overtop of me while I sit against the wall? That way we can kiss each other while we press our bodies together–"

"Yes," she said. "That sounds perfect. And it will be easier for you to tell me what to do next."

"Possibly. But something tells me you'll pretty soon figure out what to do entirely on your own. But first, take off the rest of your clothes so I can feel *all* of you up next to me."

"Mmm, yes," she purred. "I want to feel every square inch of your body next to me."

While the two of us peeled off our tops and shoes, I could hear West pulling his pants off his ankles and spreading his legs in a wide 'V' on the floor of the elevator. This time, he didn't want anything getting in the way of his enjoying himself while he imagined the two of us making love in the dark.

"Okay," I said, when I heard the last piece of clothing drop to the floor. "Come over here and sit on my lap. I want to feel your wet pussy rubbing up against me."

"Fuck, yes," she growled, swinging her legs over my hips and lowering herself on top of my thighs.

She leaned forward, pressing her tits against mine, and we locked lips as our tongues danced in each other's mouths.

"Mmm," she moaned, twisting her hips on my lap.

I could feel her mound rubbing against abdomen as a trickle of liquid ran down the front of my stomach. I lifted my hands and squeezed her tits, plunging my tongue deeper into her mouth. Elle wriggled her hips over the space between my thighs, trying vainly to get direct stimulation to her burning clit. I reached under her ass and slipped three fingers inside her pussy, and she began to hop up and down on me like a kangaroo.

"Yes, Jade," she panted. "Fuck me with your hand. I want to feel *every* part of you..."

As I listened to the sound of her sopping pussy ramming against my hand, I angled my wrist and pinched her clit between my other two fingers. She pressed her hips harder against my mound and I began to roll her hard button between my fingers.

"*Oh fuck*, Jade," she hissed. "That feels so good. Rub my

clit while I fuck your fingers. You're going to make me come very soon..."

Although I wanted to stimulate myself while she rubbed her body against me, with my legs held closed by her vice-grip of my thighs, I decided to give all of my dedicated attention to her.

"Yes, Elle," I purred, slipping down the wall a few inches so I could suck on her tits while she writhed against my dripping hand. "Come for me, baby. I want to feel your pussy squeezing my fingers when you let it loose."

As I sucked on her hard teats, burying my face between her plump tits, Elle suddenly arched her body and wailed at the top of her lungs.

"I'm cumming, Jade!" she screamed. "Suck my tits while I cum all over your sweet pussy!'

The walls of her pussy tightened, contracting over my fingers, and much to my delight and surprise, she began squirting out of her hole all over my mound. With her juices suddenly spraying over my clit, I lurched my body forward as a powerful orgasm suddenly washed over me. While we mashed our tits together and sucked on each other's tongues, I heard West groaning on the other side of the elevator as he flapped his hand wildly against his raging hard-on.

Moments later, the sound of clanging metal began emanating from far beneath us in the elevator shaft. But this time, the banging didn't have any rhythm to it, sounding more like the noise revelers make when they celebrate a new year by thumping pots together. Apparently, our fellow captives had heard the sounds of ecstasy echoing through the shaft and were signaling their approval of our little distraction.

4

———

Elle remained seated on my lap for many more minutes while we continued kissing and I caressed her wet labia with the tips of my fingers. It felt wonderful to have given her such a satisfying first lesbian experience, and I reveled in the feeling of her dripping pussy pressed against mine as our sweaty bodies rested against one another.

After a while, she pulled back a few inches and peered at me in the darkness.

"Thank you for making love to me so tenderly," she said. "I never imagined it could be this good. But what about you? This whole time you were focused on me. I want to touch you in the same places and make you feel as good as you did to me."

I smiled, running my fingers through her hair softly.

"I enjoyed that as much as you did Elle, don't you worry. When two women make love, it's more about the journey than the destination. We don't always have to get off to enjoy the experience of loving one another."

"I can see that," Elle said, lowering her head down the

front of my chest. "But I've never felt a woman that way and I want this as much as you. Don't you want to feel my lips touching *you* now?"

I grabbed Elle's hair, holding her gently against my stomach.

"I do," I said, imagining her joined with me in a different way. "But not *that* way just yet. I want to feel your lips touching me in a different place."

"A different place?"

"I want to *fuck* you this time instead of making love to you. I want to feel your pussy rubbing against mine when we come together."

"Oh my God," Elle panted. "Yes, Jade. That sounds unbelievably sexy. What's the best way–"

I smiled as a devious thought crossed my mind. Up to this point, I'd felt a little guilty leaving West to his own devices, and I knew he and Elle were just waiting for an excuse to come closer together.

"I want you to get on all fours, facing away from me," I said. "I'll turn the other way around while we rub our asses together."

"But how–"

"Just trust me on this," I said. "I think you're going to like this. We won't just be rubbing our *asses* together."

"Oh," she said, quickly lifting herself off me and positioning herself a few feet away from me in West's direction.

I just hoped he hadn't spent himself entirely listening us making love the last time.

"How are you doing over there, West?" I said. "Do you think you can keep yourself amused a little longer while Elle and I try something a little different?"

"Knock yourselves out," he grinned. "I could do this all

day and all night if necessary. I haven't been this hard for this long in ages."

"Don't lose that thought," I said. "We might be able to find some use for a *real* cock soon enough. Save a bit for us when the time comes."

"I'm not going anywhere," he said. "And neither is my dick."

I smiled as I positioned our clothes beneath the two of us, placing my hands and the balls of my feet on the floor, facing away from Elle. Then I shifted my weight backward until our cheeks touched.

"Mmm," Elle purred as she swiveled her buttocks playfully against mine. "I like the feel of your ass touching mine."

"That's not the *only* thing you're going to feel," I said, tilting my hips downward as my wet pussy caressed the inside of her thighs.

"Fuck, yes," Elle panted as she lifted her ass to press her vulva against mine. "This is so hot. I can feel your lips touching mine. Fuck me with your pussy. I want to feel you gushing against me again."

"Mmm," I said, mashing our cunts together. With our vulvas coated in slippery juices, as we slid our pussies against one another, a different kind of slopping sound filled the compartment.

"Fuck *me*..." West groaned, inches away from Elle's face with her body positioned near the base of his legs.

I could only imagine what was going through his mind as he listened to Elle and me fucking each other, and I smiled at how prescient his words were about to be.

Soon enough, West, I grinned.

As Elle and I gnashed our pussies together feeling our wet labia sliding over each other, I pressed myself harder against her clit, sliding her further in West's direction. Even though I was lost in the moment fucking her so hard, I had a second agenda for pushing her across the floor. I estimated that she was now only a few inches away from West's throbbing hard-on.

"Look between your legs, Elle," I said. "Even though we can't see each other in the dark, imagine you're watching our pussies rub together and seeing my tits shaking while I make love to you."

"Yes–" she said, then suddenly stopped, with our labia locked in a slippery kiss.

I sensed she'd felt something *else* in the darkness, and I knew her mind was racing about what to do next. But it didn't take long to begin hearing the sound of slurping noises coming from West's side of the elevator, as he began to groan excitedly.

"Oh God, Elle," he hissed. "That feels incredible. I've wanted you for so long..."

As he began thrusting his hips rhythmically into Elle's eager mouth, she hummed in pleasure while I resumed grinding against her pussy.

Knowing that the three of us were joined together in an erotic daisy chain ratcheted my passion to a higher level. As we all began to moan and whine in tandem, my body suddenly tensed up and I squirted hard between Elle's legs, spraying my juices all over her tits and her face impaled on West's pole. She groaned loudly with West's dick in her mouth, then I felt her buttocks spasming against mine as her body quivered in the throes of another powerful climax. At the same time, West began grunting in rhythmic sequence, jetting his cum deep inside Elle's mouth. The sound of the three of us moaning in mutual pleasure must have been music to the ears of the listening gallery a few floors beneath us, and I wondered if they might soon get the same idea that we had.

Suddenly I no longer cared if anyone came to our rescue for the next few hours. We were having way too much fun finding ways to pass the time on our own little fantasy island.

5

_____

For a few moments, we all remained still while we listened to the sound of the three of us panting in the darkness. This time there was no fanfare from others locked in the elevator shaft, now lost in their own distractions. Elle lifted herself off West's dripping cock and shuffled her body back over the floor, resting her back on the wall next to me. I reached out my hand and we interlocked our fingers, squeezing our hands together in acknowledgement of what had just happened.

Nobody wanted to say anything, embarrassed in the way lovers sometimes are the morning after an impassioned night of drunken partying. After all, we didn't really know each other very well, we were simply victims of the strange circumstance we'd found ourselves in.

It's funny the way a crisis brings people together, I thought.

I was about to break the silence when the sound of a distant voice suddenly perked our ears. As we lay still in the darkened elevator, the unmistakable sound of a woman moaning wafted into our chamber. But this time, the noise had a distinct cadence to it, like two bodies slamming up against a metal wall.

"Yes, yes!" the woman said. "Fuck me hard, Chase!"

I smiled, realizing we'd aroused the interest of more than our little group.

"It seems that we've started a chain reaction," West chuckled from the other side of the elevator.

"What else are people going do when they're locked up in close quarters for such a long period of time?" I said.

"It *is* kind of exciting," Elle mused. "Being stuck in the darkness, feeling our way around with a bunch of strangers..."

"I'd hardly say we qualify as *strangers* anymore," West said.

The woman's voice suddenly grew louder and more forceful.

"Oh God, Chase!" she hollered. "Pound my ass!"

"That's certainly *one* way to get to know each other better," I laughed.

"I can't believe I'm admitting this," Elle said. "But I'm actually getting turned on listening to all this sex in the darkness."

The woman's voice reached a crescendo as the banging noises echoed through the shaft.

"I'm coming baby!" she wailed. "Uhn! Uhn! Uhn!"

"Me too," I said. "What about you West? Do you think you have any ammunition left in your cartridge?"

I could hear the shuffling of clothes, as West reached for something to clean himself up with.

"I don't know what it is about this situation," he said, "but I haven't been this turned on since I was a teenager. It's like I'm thirteen years old again. My cock hasn't been this resilient in twenty years!"

"We shouldn't let all that energy go to waste," I said. "What do you think, Elle? Are you ready for some more fun and games?"

"I'm so horny, I could fuck a billy-goat right about now," she said.

I smiled, sensing the opportunity to bring the two colleagues closer together.

"I suspect you've got something a little better endowed on the other side of the elevator. I can feel the sexual energy between you two. If you don't fuck each other soon, there's liable to be a short-circuit in here before long."

"You're probably right," Elle said. "But what about you? What will you do to keep yourself distracted?"

"I'll let my fantasies wander for a little while," I said. I picked up the Osé vibrator resting on top of my skirt and slid it across the inside of Elle's thighs. "I've got my little friend here to keep me amused. You two go get yourselves better acquainted. I'll be just fine for a little while."

"Okay," she said. "But don't get too attached to that thing. I'm looking forward to tasting you with my *own* tongue when I'm finished with West."

"I'll be waiting patiently," I smiled. "Dreaming of all the ways we can pleasure one another."

"Mmm," she said. "Save that thought. I'll be back soon."

"Don't rush things too much," I said. "I'll be enjoying myself just as much as the two of you."

Elle kissed me sweetly on the lips, then skittered over to West's side of the elevator. Moments later, I heard the sound of wet lips kissing and two voices moaning. From the rustling sounds, I guessed that West had remained seated while Elle had assumed the superior position, sitting on his lap.

This time, she won't have to fish around for something to

stimulate her pussy, I smirked in the darkness. As I imagined her sinking down over West's pole, I plunged the Osé vibrator into my pussy and began rocking my hips back and forth.

"Ohh," Elle moaned as the sound of rhythmic thumping emanated from the other side of the elevator.

"Elle," West panted. "I've wanted this for so long. You feel so good."

"I've been watching you for quite some time," she sighed. "I had no idea you were so well equipped."

"Uhnn," West groaned, slapping his balls against Elle's ass.

"Fuck me with your big dick, West," Elle grunted. "Let's give Jade something to think about."

"Oh, I'm *thinking* about it, alright," I said, tapping the button on the bottom of the Osé, activating it's tongue action. "I'm already fantasizing about what I want to do with the two of you when you're done over there."

"Do you want a piece of West's cock too?" Elle said.

"Maybe," I teased. "It depends on whether I'll have a pretty girl to play with at the same time."

"Mmm, yes," Elle said. "Do you think you might *like* that, West? Having your way with both of us at the same time?"

"*Fuck*, Elle," he panted. "I'm trying to keep it together. Don't make me pop off too soon. That's the last thing I need floating around the office when we get back to work. That I couldn't even last long enough to satisfy you–"

"Don't worry, West," Elle purred. "Your secret will be safe with me. Just imagine sliding your cock between our pussies while we rub our bodies together..."

"Oh God..." West groaned as his mind began to wander.

"Yes, baby," Elle said. "Come inside me as you imagine the two of us tribbing your big cock between our wet lips..."

I smiled at Elle's torment of poor West. But I sensed she was trying to excite someone *else* in the room, and it was working. As I squirmed against the pulsing wand and the slippery tongue caressing my pussy, I couldn't resist getting in on the action.

"Fuck, yes," I hissed. "I want to feel some *real* meat between my legs next time, Elle. I want to feel his pole trembling as he comes all over the two of us–"

"*Damn*," West groaned, as Elle pressed her ass down over his balls. "I can't stop it–"

"Yes, baby," Elle purred. "I feel you cumming inside me. Let it go while you dream about your fantasy supermodels. It's about to happen for real."

"Ohh!" I groaned, pressing the Osé toy harder against me as I began cumming in unison with West. "I feel it too. My cock is twitching inside me too. I'm cumming imagining it's *your* cock fucking me right now, West. Come with me, baby."

"*Uhnn, uhnn, uhnn,*" West grunted, as Elle's pussy squeezed his pulsating dick.

By the time he finished moaning, I'd soaked the wet floor and clothes in front of me.

"Holy shit!" I sighed, sliding down the wall in contentment. "That was fucking hot! You two sure know how to drive a girl crazy."

"We're just getting started," Elle said, squeezing West's throbbing cock with the walls of her pussy. "I can feel that West is up for some more fun. It's time the three of us finally came together. Why don't you come over here and join us, Jade?"

"I thought you'd never ask," I said, sliding my body over to their side of the elevator.

I reached my hands out to find them in the dark and felt Elle's back as she sat straddled West's hips with his back against the elevator wall. I spread my knees over his legs and shimmied my body against them, pressing my breasts against Elle's sweaty back.

"Mmm," she purred. "You're so warm."

"And wet," West said, feeling my juices running over the top of his thighs.

"All the better to *fuck* you with," I said, reaching behind my ass to squeeze his balls. "Are you still hard? Because we're not done with you yet."

Elle turned her head to kiss me as she flexed her buttocks, gripping West's pole.

"Oh he's hard alright. But I want to get my hands on you before he gets any ideas. I've been dying to taste you since the moment I laid eyes on you."

"Really?" I said. "I thought you were just into men?"

"So did I until I saw you. There was something about the way you looked at us with that gleam in your eye. I knew I couldn't let you get away the moment the elevator doors closed."

"I guess the power failure happened at a fortuitous time then," I chuckled.

"It's the best thing that could have happened to us," West nodded.

I reached around Elle's back and squeezed her tits gently.

"So how do you want to do this? We better act fast before West loses that loving feeling."

"If you *really* want a piece of him," she said. "I suppose I can let you have first dibs–"

I smiled at Elle's offer, but I had other ideas for West's tool.

"I think we can find a way for him to get in on the action while we still have our way with each other."

"Really?" Elle said. "I'm not picturing it. How can we–"

"Never fear," I said. "I've had a bit more practice with these situations. Get back on the floor on all fours."

"But West has already–"

"Don't you worry about him. He's about to have the experience of his life. I'll lie underneath you in a sixty-nine position so we can lick each other at the same time."

"But I thought you said–" West protested.

"There's plenty in it for you *too*, West" I said. "Get behind Elle's ass and play with her from behind. That way, we can both have access to your boy parts."

Elle lifted herself off West's staff and positioned herself over top of our jumble of clothes. I slithered underneath her, grabbing the sides of her thighs, pulling my head between her splayed knees. West patted the floor with his hands trying to locate us and when he felt Elle's ass turned up in the air, he positioned himself behind her.

I reached up feeling for his dick and when I grasped his manhood, I gasped. It was bigger than I imagined, at least eight inches in length and six inches around. As I stroked my fingers toward its apex, I smiled when I felt his slippery head. He was still coated in Elle's juices and I plopped it into my mouth, savoring her delicious scent.

"Hmm," I hummed, swirling my tongue around his corona.

Elle could feel my breath blowing out of my nostrils toward her exposed pussy and she lowered herself toward my face, desperate to feel my touch. I pulled West's cock out of my mouth and rubbed the tip against her clit, licking his shaft from the base of his balls all the way to the tip, slathering my tongue over both of their glans.

"Oh God," West panted in delirious pleasure, feeling two

women's bodies caressing his sensitive organ for the first time.

"Lick my clit, Jade," Elle growled, elated to feel my mouth against her sex finally. "Make West cum all over my pussy."

"I'd rather feel you come on my tongue," I cooed. "I've got other ideas for West."

I grabbed his shaft and angled the tip toward Elle's hole, and he eagerly sank his manhood into her tunnel. While they both groaned feeling my breath on their genitals, Elle spread her thighs further apart, lowering her vulva closer to my face. I pressed my hands outward against the inside of her knees until her flaming clit touched my lips. As I sucked her nub into my mouth and swirled my tongue over her shaft, she buckled under the weight.

"Oh my God, Jade," she hissed. "That feels incredible. Suck my clit while West fucks my pussy. I've never felt anything this good..."

As West rammed his cock in and out of Elle's hole, I felt his balls swinging against my forehead and I raised my hands to cup his sac, stroking the space in front of his anus.

"Fuckkk!" he squealed, hardly believing he was the lucky recipient of both our attention.

He leaned forward and grabbed Elle's tits from behind, pressing her face closer toward my steaming pussy. Smelling my box inches from her lips, she placed her head between my legs and began licking me like a puppy. As West began pounding her faster, I swung my arms around her hips and pulled her harder into my crotch. The thrusting motion accentuated the stimulation of my clit, as her tongue slapped back and forth against my inflamed nub.

"Mmm," I moaned, feeling Elle's clit growing harder in my mouth. "Suck my cunt, Elle. I want to feel you cum in my mouth as I squirt all over your face."

Elle nodded enthusiastically, trying to mimic the stimulation I was giving her on the other end. She was a quick study, and before long I felt my orgasm approaching as West's balls suddenly tightened and Elle began bucking wildly on top of my face. Within seconds, all three of us were wailing at the top of our lungs, signaling we'd reached the height of pleasure.

As Elle's clit began twitching in my mouth, I grabbed West's balls and squeezed them tightly while he tensed his buttocks and came inside Elle for the second time that day. I could feel his pelvic floor muscle contracting as he emptied his seed inside Elle's pussy, and the combination of sensations was too much for me to hold back. As Elle and West groaned in mutual climax, I tilted my hips and sprayed my juices all over Elle's face planted between my legs. We shook and grunted in unison for what seemed like a full minute before collapsing together on the floor in exhaustion.

But just as I was looking forward to a relaxing respite in the arms of my new friends, the elevator suddenly lurched and the lights came on as it began to descend.

"Holy shit!" Elle said, realizing we only had seconds before the doors opened and we'd be exposed to anyone waiting on the ground floor. "We better get ourselves put together before we're found out!"

We scrambled to put on our wet and wrinkly clothes, and as the elevator jerked to a stop, we looked at each other and smiled.

"That was one hell of a ride," Elle grinned.

As the elevator doors opened, we grabbed each other's hands and nonchalantly strode past the alarmed maintenance crew and rescue workers. The large wet spots and undeniable scent of sex on our clothes left little doubt what we'd been up to in the elevator. When we swung open the main exit doors and walked out onto the building courtyard, a large crowd was waiting to greet us. Without skipping a beat, they spontaneously erupted into a loud ovation.

I guess we weren't the only ones being entertained while we were locked up this whole time, I grinned.

Elle and West peered at one another, then leaned over and kissed each other passionately. I was happy to see that I'd been able to create more than one new connection among my friends at the Ogilvy & Mather Advertising Agency.

Everybody's an exhibitionist in disguise...

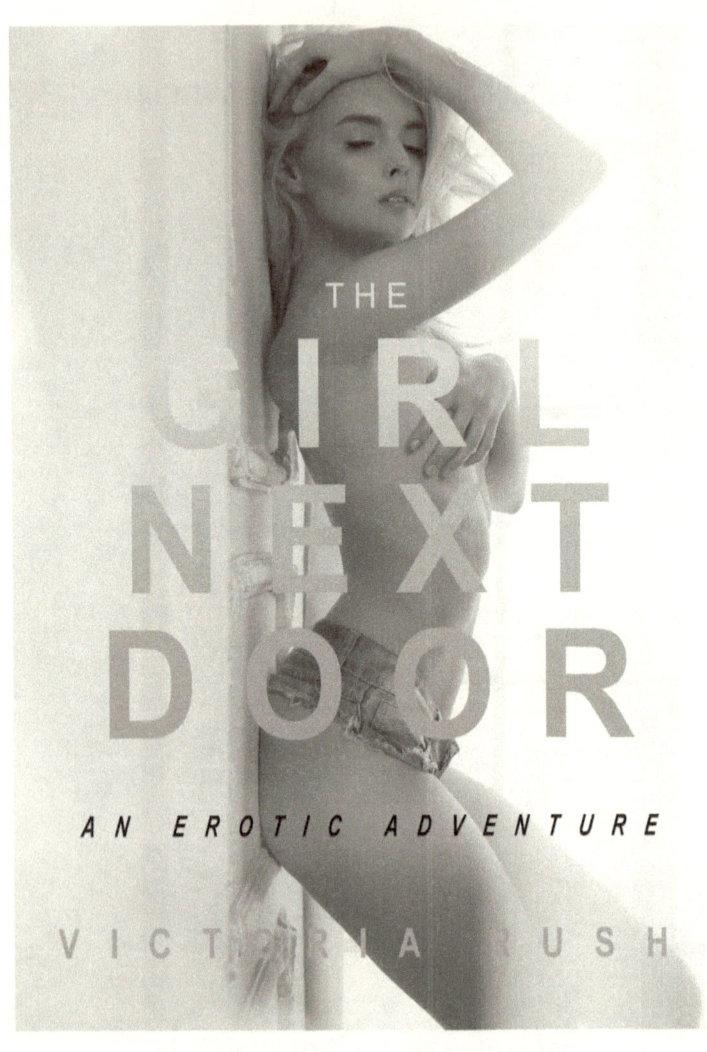

Spying on the neighbors just got a lot more interesting...

Everything's sexier in the dark...

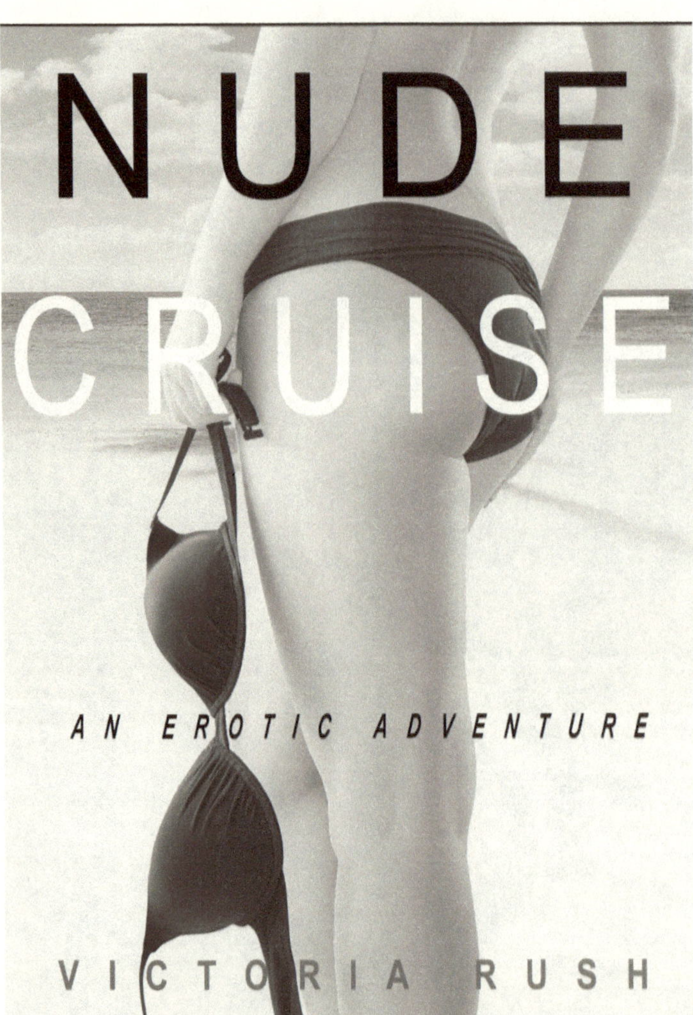

Some people get wet on a cruise for different reasons...

Books 1 -5 in the bestselling series - 60% off

THE DINNER PARTY - PREVIEW
FINGER FOOD

Sometime later, I heard a soft tap on my bedroom door. Not wanting to remove myself just yet from my cocoon of luxury, I called out to answer.

"Yes?"

"It's time for your massage," a woman's voice replied.

"Just one minute please."

I reluctantly stepped out of the bath and quickly toweled myself dry. I wrapped a large bath sheet around me, re-donned my mask, then opened the bedroom door.

A petite young Asian girl greeted me, wearing a kimono similar to mine and a crimson masquerade mask.

Apparently not everybody who works here always walks around stark naked.

The girl was utterly breathtaking. Long jet-black hair cascaded over high cheekbones past pouty lips, her delicate collarbones peeking from the top of her kimono. I could see her breasts and hips outlined by the tightly-wrapped kimono and suddenly wished that she too had come to my boudoir naked.

"My name is Jasmine," she said. "I'm your personal

masseuse and esthetician. Are you ready for your final preparation?

Just the thought of this beauty laying her tender hands on me sent a shiver down my spine.

"Definitely. Please come in. How would you like me to prepare?"

"Come with me, please."

Jasmine led me into the bathroom, where she nonchalantly removed her kimono and hung it behind the bathroom door.

Oh my God.

I didn't think anyone in this place could get more beautiful or sensuous. Jasmine had perfectly shaped B-cup breasts with a thin indentation running down the center of her perfectly toned stomach. Like everyone else in this place, her pubis was utterly bald and flawless. She barely looked eighteen and I was just about to ask her age, but she spoke first.

"If you'd like to remove your towel and lay face down on the table, we can get started. May I call you Jade?"

There was something about her confident manner and tone that belied her youthful appearance. I had no inhibitions whatsoever about displaying myself unclothed to this stranger.

"Yes, thank you, Jasmine." I unhooked my bath sheet and threw it against the side of the tub.

"Would you like me to drape your backside?" Jasmine asked.

"That won't be necessary," I quickly answered.

Jasmine walked over to the vanity counter and picked up two small bottles of oil resting under an orange radiant lamp. She brought them back to the massage table, opened one, and poured the oil into one cupped hand then rubbed her hands together. The scent of lavender wafted toward my nose.

I closed my eyes in anticipation of her touch. I'd had massages before, but nothing as sensuous and stimulating as this. When her hands touched the small of my back, I jerked reflexively from the sexual tension. My heart was beating a hundred miles an hour as I felt the blood coursing through my veins.

Jasmine must have sensed my nervous tension and began pressing her fingers more firmly into my back as she moved them slowly up each side of my spine. The warm oil allowed her hands to glide effortlessly across my skin. She used every surface of her hands to massage my muscles, expertly kneading my skin with her fingers and palm.

I began to relax as my muscles softened and surrendered to her touch. She sensuously massaged every part of my back, shoulders, and neck, applying just the right amount of pressure. Periodically, she would pour more warm oil on my lower back, dipping her hands in it to replenish the silky lubrication against my pliant skin.

Just as the sexual tension began to subside from the utter relaxation of the massage, Jasmine moved her hands down to my buttocks and began to caress them in soft circular motions. My glutes contracted involuntarily and I unconsciously pressed my mound into the firm padding of the table. Suddenly I was quickly reminded that a gorgeous young woman was caressing my naked body. She cupped each buttock between her hands as she massaged my ass tantalizingly, her little finger sliding slowly into the cleft just above my anus.

Periodically, I'd partially open one of my eyes with my head turned in her direction to look at her gorgeous body. My head was at the same level as her midsection, and my mouth watered as I watched her stomach muscles flex and her hips undulate with each movement of her hands. At times her pussy was almost right beside me and I wanted to reach out and run my own fingers up her soft legs.

I was in total heaven and getting wetter by the moment. Just when I thought I couldn't stand it anymore, she suddenly moved her hands down to my feet and began massaging her thumbs into my soles.

I'd always loved having my feet massaged, but nobody did it like Jasmine. She cradled my foot and used every part of her hands to massage and knead every surface from my heel to my toes. I didn't want her to stop, but there were other parts of my body that were screaming for attention.

As if reading my thoughts, she began moving her hands up toward my calf, using her thumbs to spread the muscle apart. She lingered almost as long on my calf as she had on my foot, rolling the ball of my calf between both of her hands, sliding her slick hands up and down erotically. I couldn't help imagining how she might use those same hands to massage a man's erect cock in a similar manner. My mind wandered again to what pleasures lay in wait for me over dinner.

After shifting her hands to my right leg and giving my other foot and calf similar attention, she placed each hand just behind my knees and began to slowly move them up towards my buttocks. Her thumbs pressed against my inner thighs as she glided tantalizingly close to my apex.

I rolled my legs outward in an invitation to move closer. My legs were parted enough that I was sure she could see my vulva from her vantage point behind me. In my highly aroused state, my lips were engorged and spread apart, revealing my moist and quivering opening.

But as much as I desperately wanted her to, Jasmine

never touched me there. She repeatedly slid her hands right up to the edge of my slit, pressing and rotating her thumbs on the fleshy meat of my upper thighs just below my aching pussy. I suppose this was part of her master plan—to tease me mercilessly and inflame my passions so I'd be ready for just about anything at the main event.

It was certainly working. After thirty minutes of Jasmine's ministrations, I was grinding my pussy into the table trying desperately to give my clit some needed direct stimulation.

Just when I thought I couldn't be teased any more tantalizingly, Jasmine opened one of the bottles of warm oil and poured it directly into the crack of my ass. She paused as the fluid flowed down and directly over my parted lips. I almost came from the gentle movement of the warm liquid as it trickled across the folds of my labia, channeled toward the junction where they joined together at my clit. I shuddered in pleasure at the feeling, even if it was only the subtlest of touch.

Jasmine suddenly interrupted my thoughts.

"Would you like to turn over now?"

It was the first time she had spoken directly to me since the massage started, and it surprised me in my catatonic, pre-orgasmic state. I practically flipped over like a fish out of water and spread my legs expectantly. Finally, I'd get some relief. Surely, she couldn't leave me hanging like this.

"It's time for your final grooming," she said. "I'll need you to part your legs a bit further to provide full access."

Grooming? I knew this was part of the process, but somehow it didn't seem fair to transition at this precise moment. At least I'd be able to stay on the comfortable massage table instead of the clinical vinyl chairs used by my regular esthetician.

Jasmine walked over to another cabinet by the makeup table and withdrew a leather bag from one of the drawers, then brought it back to the table. She reached into the bag and pulled out a cordless hair trimmer.

"Do you have a preference regarding your appearance?" she asked. "Do you prefer natural, neatly trimmed, or bare?"

I knew she was referring to my pubic hair, which I generally kept neatly trimmed. I'd always thought going fully bald was unnatural and unseemly, catering to men's prurient fantasies of fucking young schoolgirls. But in this situation, it seemed entirely appropriate, like I was stripping away all my camouflage and armor.

If tonight was all about being watched, I might as well bare myself in every sense of the word and truly let my inhibitions go. I began to fantasize about rubbing my bare pussy against Jasmine's while she poured warm oil between us. The more work she had to do on me, the more chance I'd have to make this last and hopefully get off.

I didn't hesitate. "Bare, thank you."

"As you wish," she said. "I'll remove the long hairs first with the trimmer, then shave you smooth with a razor."

No waxing? This was different. I was relieved to not have to bear the painful and violent trial of having my hairs ripped out en masse. Although shaving down there was always a scary proposition, I felt safe in the capable and practiced hands of this beautiful esthetician.

Jasmine nodded, then flipped a switch on the trimmer. The device buzzed softly as she placed it gently on my mound. I had only a light dusting of fur and it didn't take long for her to remove it with a few short strokes over my pubis. I shuddered as the vibrations penetrated deep into my core. If she had placed the flat head on my clitoris, I would have popped off in a millisecond. Instead, she turned the trimmer face-down and gently swiped the vibrating teeth against the sides of my vulva, sensuously separating my labia with her hands as she moved the device between my legs to trim the hairs on the inside and outside of my labia.

It was an insanely titillating feeling, but just clinical enough to bring me down from my plateau and shift my focus. My mind wandered to the upcoming feast, and I contemplated what surprises lay in wait at the main event. The hostesses had suggested there would be 'contact' of some sort during the meal, and I was intrigued exactly who and how it would be administered. The idea of being fully bald, cleansed, and thoroughly stimulated going into the event was an incredible rush.

Jasmine continued with the trimmer all the way down my perineum to my anus, barely touching me with the trimmer so as not to pinch any delicate tissues. Apparently there were no parts of my erogenous zone that would remain untouched, now—and perhaps later.

She turned off the trimmer and placed it at the foot of the table. Then she took a bottle of gel from the bag and spread the gel on her hands. Using both hands, she spread it gently between my legs, starting on my mound all the way down to my rosebud.

My body almost levitated above the table as Jasmine finally laid her hands directly on my clitoris. The gel had a mild stinging quality that added to the stimulating sensation. If this was meant to excite my follicles in preparation for the shave, it wasn't the only feature of my anatomy that it made erect. I could feel the hood of my clitoris retract as my button filled with blood and began to push outward. Suddenly, I was fully stimulated again and lusting for Jasmine's touch. I fantasized about her bending down and taking my swollen nub between her puffy lips and letting me come in her mouth.

Unfortunately, my satisfaction would have to wait a little longer. Instead, Jasmine reached into her bag and pulled out a straight-edge razor. In anyone else's hands, it might look threatening, especially in my prostrated and vulnerable position. But something about the way she delicately and sensuously opened the jackknifed tool instantly evaporated my fears. I could see how this type of razor would in fact give her better control safely cutting my stubs instead of the usual ladies plastic razor.

With her right hand, Jasmine gently laid the razor on its flat edge at the top of my mound, while she gently pulled my skin upwards with her other hand. Then she slowly turned the sharp edge perpendicular to my skin and began softly scraping the razor downwards. I could hear the bristling sound as the razor edge removed my nubs right down to the follicles. She repeated the pattern in one inch wide swipes on one side then the other of my pubis, being ever-so-careful to stop just where my clitoris lay quivering in a mixture of fear and excitement. There was something about the utter vulnerability of the procedure that made it the most erotic experience I'd ever had.

Jasmine used the same deft touch as she moved down my vulva and perineum, scraping the vestiges of stray hairs away with gentle swipes of the long blade, while sensuously separating my folds and flesh with her other hand. She took extra time and care around my anus and clit, using the gentlest and slowest motion I've ever felt someone apply to my body. The combination of fright and titillation as she probed my most sensitive body parts created a river of sensuous fluids running down my vulva. By this time, no shaving gel was necessary to provide a smooth gliding surface for the knife.

When she was finished, Jasmine retrieved a fresh wash towel from beside the sink and held it under the warm water faucet then twisted the excess water into the basin. She returned to the table and placed it over my splayed legs then gently cleansed the excess moisture and remaining shaving gel with gentle massaging movements of her hands. The warm, moist towel felt exquisite against my newly shaved skin. Jasmine's hands now felt comforting between my legs rather than erotic.

She had taken me on an incredibly sensuous erotic arc, right to the edge of ecstasy and back, to a quiet relaxed place. I exhaled fully and completely for the first time in almost an hour.

Jasmine removed the towel from between my legs and held up a large hand mirror at a forty-five degree angle toward me.

"What do you think?" she asked.

I tilted my head up and studied her masterpiece. Far from the usual red and swollen vulva that I typically experienced after the violent waxing with my regular esthetician, I'd never seen my pussy look so beautiful. Utterly bereft of any hair, my entire perineum from my pubic mound to my anus was totally bald, pink—and gorgeous. I just stared at my beautiful pussy, utterly transfixed by the transformation.

"You have to *feel* it to really appreciate how beautiful you are, Jade," Jasmine purred.

I moved my right hand down, running my fingers along the edges of my pussy. I gasped from a feeling I'd never felt before. It felt smooth as silk: no bumps or blemishes or cuts or bruises. It was almost as if I was feeling somebody else— somebody I'd never felt before. I couldn't stop my left hand joining the other in rubbing and caressing my sensitive organs.

Jasmine lowered the mirror and smiled at me as I felt the moisture begin to accumulate between my legs again.

"It's almost time for your dinner appointment," she said. "Why don't you save the best for last? I think you'll find plenty of ways to satisfy your appetite over the next couple of hours."

She lifted my kimono from the hook at the edge of the bathtub and held it open for me.

"I'll escort you downstairs now if you're ready. All you need to bring is your kimono and slippers—and your mask of course."

I sat up slowly and stepped off the massage table. Turning around, I held my arms out as Jasmine lifted one arm of the silk robe onto me then the other. Then she turned around to face me, wrapped the silk tie around me, and tied a single bow over my belly button. She retrieved my matching silk slippers and knelt down on one knee to gently lift my feet one at a time and place them softly inside. It took every ounce of my power not to grab her head and pull it into my pulsating pussy.

Jasmine stood up gracefully and smiled into my eyes.

"If you'll follow me, I'll escort you now to the fantasy feast."

She didn't bother putting her own robe on. Her tight little ass barely jiggled as she stepped smartly ahead of me. I wasn't sure if I'd have a chance to feel Jasmine's touch again before the evening was over, but for now I was in total bliss ogling her petite, curvaceous figure from behind...

Read More

ABOUT THE AUTHOR

If you would like to receive notification of new book(s) in Jade's Erotic Adventures, follow me at http://bookbub.com/authors/victoria-rush.

If you have a moment, please post a brief review on my Amazon book page at viewbook.at/elevatorshaft. Even just a couple of sentences will help other readers find and enjoy this book as much as you hopefully did.

Follow, share, like, and comment at:

www.facebook.com/authorvictoriarush
www.pinterest.com/authorvictoriarush
www.twitter.com/authorvictoriarush
authorvictoriarush@outlook.com

Hope to see you again soon!